BEST SERVED COLD

BOB SCHOONOVER

"This story does a good job of investing in the background and in the characters. A very fun story to read."

J Dark, author of *Best Intentions*

"Definitely worth the ride. It will make you wonder about companies and their priorities."

L. A. Jacob, author of *Grimaulkin*

"This tightly-wound drama serves up the vile taste of the profits-are-all motive lurking in the depths of American capitalism, with a bitter chaser to remind you: Beware the anger of a patient man."

Vanessa MacLaren-Wray, author of *All That Was Asked*

"An evocative and chilling tale of a man pushed too far by the uncaring greed of the corporation he works for. It makes you wonder: How far would you go?"

Steven Radecki, author of *Building Baby Brother*

"A bone-chilling tale about the greed of corporate executives, their bad judgement and callused decisions, that ends with a horrifying conclusion that makes you question whether the end justifies the means."

Steve Soult, author of *Reduction in Force*

"A personal and deeply provocative tale that encapsulates in science fiction what corporations could do today — and the extreme to which an individual might need to go to seek justice. A captivating read from start to finish."

Ryan Southwick, author of *Angels in the Mist*

"Well-constructed, imaginative, and, quite frankly, terrifying. It is, truly, a corporate horror story. I read it, caught up in the plot, 'savoring' every passage, from the outstanding title to the last word."

Nancy Wood, author of *Due Date*

BEST SERVED COLD

S TEVEN BROOKS HAD ALWAYS THOUGHT OF HIMSELF as a quiet and patient man. It was unimaginable to him that he could be pushed beyond the limits of his tolerance and compassion into killing anyone. But that was the Steven Brooks of three days ago. This Friday noontime found him standing to the side of a lavish dining room humming his wife's favorite tune while he watched corporation owners dine on food that he had specially prepared for them.

The path Steven's life had taken to that Friday noontime began with some anticipation on a Friday exactly three months earlier. Reginald Gessler, the RIZALTID Corporation Vice President for Human Resources, had posted a notice that the two hundred and seventy-seven lower-tier headquarters employees would be receiving a special bonus in the company cafeteria that afternoon.

At the announced time, Steven found himself queued up behind his immediate supervisor, Amelia Roberts, an attractive thirty-something brunette, who was head of the building's Food Services Division. "How big a bonus will we be getting?" he asked.

"I wouldn't get my hopes up for money, Steve. This is RIZALTID, after all, and the family that runs the corporation is notoriously stingy when it comes to us employees. No, it isn't money unless it's a whole bunch," Amelia replied peering ahead and pointing. "Gessler's flunkies are handing out packages of something. From the looks of people leaving the table up front, this is probably going to be a letdown."

Steven craned his neck to look around the line at people walking away with whatever the bonus was. Amelia appeared to be right about the letdown; small clusters of people were gesturing in an unhappy manner as they quietly talked among themselves while leaving the cafeteria. Steven frowned with puzzlement as he saw many individuals cram containers of whatever they had received into large trash bins by the exit.

Apparently, some word about the bonus handout was passing down the line toward Amelia and himself from one person to the next, people shaking their heads after hearing whatever was said and leaving the line without receiving a package. The person just ahead of Amelia leaned forward to hear something then straightened and turned to leave as well. Amelia reached out a hand to stop him before he could leave.

"What's going on?" she asked.

"It's this fucking RIZALTID. Our 'bonus' is a canister of that new stuff they made a big advertising push for. Remember what we heard here in the headquarters: 'MultiNutriGood, dozens of ways to prepare and use this healthy food additive!'" He shook his head in disgust. "Probably cost them ten cents to make, and that whole canister they're so generously giving us for a so-called bonus is probably going to retail for under ten bucks. This is just a PR stunt. They make a gesture," he pointed with a thumb over his shoulder, "take photos of us getting the stuff, and use those for PR. The supposed good deal part for us is we're the first ones to get this new stuff." He shook his head again and moved away toward the exit doors.

Amelia turned and watched the man go, then looked at Steven. "You're fairly new here so you haven't seen how typical this is of the way the corporation operates. They only thing they demonstrably care about is how much profit the family owning the business can make. I imagine you were happy with the conditions of employment when you were hired, with the health care benefit, life insurance, and retirement investment, right?" Steven nodded. "But that's all through company subsidiaries, so they're actually making money off you, me, and the rest of us here." She gestured toward the table ahead of them, "This just shows how little they think of company employees."

"We don't need to be here for this photo op, so we might just as well go home." Amelia stepped out of line and turned toward the doors. "You going, or staying?"

"Staying, I guess," he said even though he was disappointed with what was being given out as a bonus. "Our budget's a little tight right now with the move here and getting settled in, so every little thing helps."

"Okay, I can understand that. Hope the MNG turns out to be as good as the advertising says. See you tomorrow."

•   •   •

"Anne, I'm home," Steven called out as he entered their two-bedroom apartment.

His wife looked up from the living room sofa and made a *shush*-ing gesture, then said in a hushed voice said, "Sally's taking a nap."

He nodded and walked over to her carrying the packaged canister that was his company bonus. Steven bent down over the back of the sofa to give his wife a light kiss then straightened and held out the package. "We got our bonus today, this new company food product. Supposed to be good stuff with lots of uses. The headquarters staff are the first ones to get this before it goes out for sale."

Anne frowned at the proffered canister. "This is the bonus you told me to expect? I was hoping for something more along the lines of cash so we could buy new clothes for Sally. She's quickly growing out of everything these days and will need more clothes soon."

"I know we could have used money, but I figured every little thing helps around here now." He shrugged. "This is what they gave out."

Sally sighed, "Steve, I love you and appreciate what you do, but that company you work for is really cheap ass."

"At least I have a job," he replied defensively.

"Yes, there is that." She nodded and reached for the package. "Let's see what the hell they gave you."

Steven handed his wife the packaged canister. "From what I read on the label it's a food supplement with vitamins and protein. It has some flavor, apparently, but not a lot, so you can add it to anything without affecting the taste much. It's supposed to be good for protein shakes, too, according to the package, and I know you like those."

"I do indeed. I need the energy to keep up with Sally these days." Anne took the package from Steven and looked at it. "Huh. 'Thousands of Uses!!!'" she read. "Think they used enough exclamation marks there? I guess I'll put this to the test and make a protein shake while you get cleaned up and change." Anne stood up. "You want one?"

Steven shook his head. "Not now, I need a beer first. Maybe later."

Anne nodded and walked into the kitchenette. "Just be quiet," she said over her shoulder. "Let Sally finish her nap."

Steven nodded and began dramatically tiptoeing toward their bedroom with a wry look on his face. Anne grinned at that and waved him on as she reached for the well-used blender that had been a wedding gift six years earlier. He heard the familiar sound of his wife humming her favorite tune as he walked into their bedroom.

Twenty-five minutes later, Steven emerged from the bedroom showered and changed, then quietly looked in on their sleeping daughter and closed her door before continuing toward the kitchen. As he neared the kitchen area Steven could look across the dining counter to see Anne had been her usual neat self, with the blender pitcher and her shake glass already washed and drying on the dish rack. A waiting beer stood next to the sink with beads of condensation on the chilled bottle. He frowned when he didn't see or hear Anne, so he paused briefly to look toward the living room, then walked around the end of the counter, intending to get his beer before he went further looking for Anne. He stopped as he rounded the corner, shocked by the sight of Anne grotesquely sprawled on her back, not moving.

"No, no, no, no ..." Steven moaned as he dropped to his knees, trying desperately to recall procedures from a first aid course he had taken years before.

He reached out to touch her neck, then leaned down to listen for any breathing. Anne didn't have a pulse and wasn't breathing; his stunned mind groped to recall half-remembered CPR procedures, and he began as best he could to resuscitate Anne.

911! He remembered he needed to call 911 right away and fumbled his phone out of the pocket of his shorts, turned it on, and set it down beside himself on the floor.

"Dial 911," he said to the phone voice assistant as he went back to his desperate life-saving efforts.

The operator quickly answered, then told him an ambulance was on the way once he briefly described Anne's state. The operator stayed on the open line with Steven, offering encouragement and providing updates on the ambulance ETA.

Seven minutes later, Steven heard an ambulance siren winding down outside his building, followed less than a minute later by loud knocking on the apartment door. Steven paused his CPR efforts to rush and open the door, then stood aside as the EMTs entered and quickly moved to Anne's side with their equipment. From the grim looks exchanged between the EMTs and their glances at him after several minutes attempting to resuscitate Anne, he suspected the worst and tried to brace himself for the news.

His efforts and those of the EMTs had been too late to save his beloved Anne.

The commotion woke Sally who sleepily stumbled into the kitchen just moments after the EMTs stopped their fruitless efforts to save Anne. Steven quickly hugged Sally while he stared down at his wife's unmoving body. Both he and his daughter began to cry.

•   •   •

The next week began in a fog of pain that slowly cleared as Steven was forced to focus on administrative matters related to Anne's death. Of necessity, Steven took the one week of paid leave he was permitted while he made his arrangements. Two particularly difficult moments for him were arranging for Anne's cremation and burial, and signing papers to claim death benefits provided through the company's insurance subsidiary.

During that week, he also made a requested visit to the coroner who had performed the autopsy on Anne. The coroner had indicated he wished to speak to Steven about his wife's death, saying he had a few questions Steven might help clear up. According to the medical examiner's death certificate, which the coroner handed to Steven, Anne's death had resulted from a 'massive cerebral hemorrhage'.

"I'm sure this is painful for you and I appreciate your willingness to speak to me," Dr. Williams, the coroner, said. "Was there anything unusual about your wife's medical history or physical condition you know of?" he asked.

Steven shook his head in reply.

"Do you know if she had been having any headaches lately or showed signs of trouble maintaining her balance, unusual stumbles for example, or even any slurred speech?"

Steven shook his head again.

"The reason I asked is that 'massive' is a greatly understated description of the degree of hemorrhage in her brain tissue. I've never seen or read about any brain hemorrhage that was so extensive without some pre-existing condition or severe head trauma. Your wife was apparently healthy. Added to that there were no physical indications or toxicology results that could explain such a severe event; so, the precipitate cause of your wife's death is a mystery. I'm not satisfied with a mystery I can't solve when it comes to anyone's death."

Steven cast a troubled looked at Williams. "You don't know what caused my wife's brain to bleed that way?"

"No. We do know what happened," the coroner replied emphasizing the 'what'. "But not why, and that bothers me."

"Could I have done anything more quickly to save her?"

"I'm sorry, but no, you couldn't have."

Steven took a deep breath and asked the most painful questions that had been going through his mind: "Was it quick, did she suffer?"

Dr. Williams clenched his jaw and said, "Are you sure you want to know?"

Steven nodded.

"Very well then," Williams went on. "Again, I'm sorry to have to tell you this. 'Quick' is a relative matter to the person suffering this way. It probably took 10 to 15 minutes from the onset of this event for your wife's body to shut down completely. Should I go on with the second part of your question? It will be more difficult to hear."

Steven nodded numbly.

The coroner reverted to a clinically detached tone and continued. "There would have been a buildup of pressure in her brain, causing pain like the worst migraine you can imagine. She would have become weak, stumbled, found it difficult to speak clearly if at all, and she would have been gasping for breath, wheezing. I know you found her on the floor, so she fell, and she probably experienced convulsions in the final moments of her life. It would have been a very painful way to die."

Steven sat there listening, contemplating the tragic final moments of his wife's life in his own painful moment.

Williams leaned forward with a sympathetic look in his eyes and placed a hand lightly on Steven's shoulder. "I am sorry," he said. "I wouldn't have told you so much the way I did, except I suspect there's something very wrong here. I just don't know what it is. If you ever come up with a clue, please let me know."

Steven nodded dully, shook Dr. Williams' hand in an automatic gesture, and left with the coroner's words, *"There's something very wrong here,"* echoing in his mind.

•　　•　　•

Since he was only allotted the one week of paid leave and couldn't afford any unpaid leave, Steven was back at work ten days after Anne's death. Two things helped him through this difficult period: his daughter, Sally, was proving to be a true source of joy in his life during the time they spent together, and at work, Amelia was an empathetic and supportive presence. Between Sally and Amelia, Steven became a bit better each day although the coroner's remarks about the mystery of Anne's death still nagged at him.

Dinners with Sally after work were an especially good time of day for him. Even though Steven was a culinary school graduate, the kitchen in their apartment had been Anne's domain, and Steven couldn't bear to spend more than an absolute minimum of time there since her death. Eating at Denny's or McDonald's every night had become part of the routine with Sally now.

Mealtimes at work helped, too. The very normalcy of life in the cafeteria further helped distract him from his distress over Anne's death. During meals Steven began to eavesdrop routinely on humorous banter and griping that made the circumstances of that time each day feel so normal. When line guys came over from the factory floor and Steven listened to them telling their jokes and swapping outlandish tales, the 'normal' often became hilarious, and Steven especially enjoyed those times.

•　　•　　•

Time passed after Anne's death — first a week, then two, then three, then a month, and then another month. Steven still felt the ache of losing his wife as well as a lingering frustration from not knowing the cause of her brain hemorrhage. Nonetheless, both the ache and frustration were muted somewhat by time and the otherwise normal circumstances of daily life.

•　　•　　•

Nearly three months after Anne died, Steven was eating lunch in the cafeteria on a Monday and noticed Reynolds, a line manager he knew slightly, sitting at a nearby table with a group of workers who seemed to know each other well. As Steven's attention was drawn to that group, he overheard Reynolds launch into a funny series of the classic 'A [fill in the blank] walked into a bar ...' type jokes that made him grin. Steven made a mental note to look for that group again when he ate in the cafeteria so he could be entertained by their humor again.

Tuesday passed without Reynolds and his cohort in the cafeteria, then Wednesday Steven came into the cafeteria for lunch and noticed Reynolds and another man Reynolds seemed to know just ahead in line. Steven finished his meal selection and looked around for Reynolds to find a seat close enough so he could listen in on the expected humorous banter. Once settled in, Steven cocked his head to one side to eavesdrop once more as he began to eat. Reynolds wasn't telling jokes today, however, and the words he was saying caught Steven's attention.

"This is totally fucked up," Steven heard Reynolds say. "It's bad enough they've been slowly replacing workers on the line with AI and robots, but when the bean counters upstairs think they're smart enough to design the factory line layout, we're really in trouble."

"Which that incident from a couple of months ago clearly shows," Reynolds's companion agreed. "Placing that line of industrial-strength poison in the same building as food production was screwed up but routing the feed for it along with that new food product through the same cluster was insane and asking for trouble."

"No shit. Trying to save a few bucks by shortening the MX-21c line and running it into an existing shared control nexus was stupid to begin with. Whoever programmed the AI that was overseeing the lines in that section had his head up his ass, too. Thank god they shut down both lines as soon as they did. If they hadn't, just after that first small MultiNutriGood batch run a few months ago that had the MX mixed into it finished, they'd have been dumping goddamn MX into ALL the MNG heading out of the building."

"No shit indeed," Reynolds's tablemate said with a nod. "From what I heard, that MX-21c is so concentrated in its base formula it's incredibly poisonous. No matter how little got into the MNG it would have made people sick."

"What's ironic about the whole thing now is they have to spend money to fix what they intended as a cost-saving measure by routing the MX through an existing control point rather than setting it up as an entirely separate production line as they should have. Since they had to disassemble and dispose of all the lines that might have been contaminated with the MX, as well as start over on the layout, it's going to cost a bunch."

"And the lines are shut down until they get everything fixed so they've lost the money they could have made from the two product lines if they hadn't had to shut them down. But you know they're going to make the fix in the quickest and cheapest way possible and hope another fuck-up doesn't happen." Reynolds paused in thought. "You think anyone's going to get in trouble over this? What they did setting things up that way was criminal."

Reynolds' companion looked around and lowered his voice. "You better watch how you say that around here. The folks upstairs would be pissed if they heard you talking that way, and you know they'd find some way to punish you."

"Anyway, nah. I heard they're '100 percent certain' they got back all the packages of contaminated MNG. That's the official line anyway from what I'm hearing. A little hard to tell apparently because some pissed off HQ folks tossed their 'bonuses', so an unknown quantity of contaminated MNG canisters went out in the trash. Seagulls at a landfill somewhere are probably dying from MX poisoning now."

He paused and looked around again, then turned back to Reynolds. "Also, from what I hear, as far as the corporation is concerned there's no evidence of contaminated MNG out there anywhere, so, no evidence, no story, and no problem. Anything that couldn't be papered over by tame lab pukes has been disappeared. It never happened, right? So, no firings." He laughed sardonically. "Can't fire an AI, anyway, can they? You think any of us are likely to talk about what we know?"

"Nope," Reynolds shook his head. "Not me for sure. You're right about what the corporate fuckheads would do. They'd can us and probably replace us with robots or AIs. They don't give a flying fuck about the people here, and I want to keep my job."

"Yeah. So, what do we do?"

"What we've been doing, the best we can," Reynolds said.

Steven sat there stunned by what he'd overheard and its implications. The first batch of MultiNutriGood, the canisters handed out as a bonus, including the one he took home to Anne, had been contaminated with whatever the hell MX-21c was? Was that MX-21c the mysterious cause of his wife's death? Had the goddamned RIZALTID Corporation killed Anne?

Steven felt a rising tide of anger at the thought and an urgent need to do something, but what could he do? How could he prove the corporation was responsible for Anne's death? And if he could, how could he make them pay for it?

Wait. He sat up, thinking. His 'bonus' canister, the one he had taken home to Anne, was it still there someplace? If it was, could he use it to prove the corporation had been responsible for Anne's death? So, find it if he could, get it tested, and see if that would solve the 'something very wrong' mystery of Anne's death.

Steven sat another moment considering his actions, then nodded to himself, stood and rapidly walked toward the cafeteria exit leaving his unfinished lunch behind. He pulled out his cell phone as he headed for the employee parking lot and called Amelia's office number.

"Amelia? ... Sorry, I need to go, emergency at home ... Yes, sorry ... No, I'm sure it will turn out all right, but I may be late coming in tomorrow ... Great ... Thanks. Bye."

Steven rushed home and directly into the kitchen, then stopped to think: where could the MNG be? He closed his eyes and concentrated, painfully trying to recall the scene in the apartment after he brought the MultiNutriGood canister home. Anne had said she would make a protein shake he recalled, and the blender pitcher and a glass had been on the drainboard, so she probably had made a shake. But he couldn't remember seeing the MNG canister on the counter afterward. In the usual neat way within her kitchen domain Anne must have put it away before she died, but where?

The canister was in the third cabinet Steven opened, neatly lined up with other staple food items on the shelf. He stood staring at it for several moments, then carefully reached for it and took it out of the cabinet. His eyesight blurred with tears as he thought about Anne and her dead body lying on the kitchen floor tiles. Losing himself in that terrible memory, Steven's grasp on the container loosened and it fell to the floor, hitting and falling on its side with the lid partly off, allowing a small amount of the powdered substance to spill onto the floor.

"Oh, shit!" he exclaimed and jumped back away from the spill. Steven looked down realizing that, if the powder was as poisonous as his dark suspicion suggested from the conversation overheard in the cafeteria, he'd have to be exceptionally careful with the way he handled it. A dust mask and latex gloves from a small storage closet in the hall would be the best he could immediately do for personal protection. He went into the hallway and got them along with a garbage bag, dustpan, and whisk broom he'd discard after sweeping up the powder. He came back into the kitchen to find Whiskers, their pet cat, licking up powder from the small spill.

"No!" Steven shouted with sufficient force to startle Whiskers and make him bolt from the room toward one of his preferred hiding places.

Steven shook his head to clear it and focus on his task as Whiskers disappeared. He took a breath. "Okay, get to it Steven," he told himself.

He'd just finished what he could for an initial cleanup and had carefully placed dustpan, whisk broom, and powder canister in the garbage bag when he heard a retching sound behind him and turned. There was Whiskers, stumbling slightly, then collapsing on his side, convulsing, and with one final twitch of his small body, lying still on the floor, just where Anne's body had been.

Steven sank to his knees staring at Whiskers' body. He was certain Whiskers was dead without needing to examine the cat, relating what Dr. Williams had described as symptoms to what he had just seen of Whisker's last moments. He slowly looked from Whiskers to the bag in his hand and was now as certain as he could be that his suspicion about the MNG was true. More tears came to Steven's eyes as he thought of this other death in his small family. He wiped at his eyes sadly reflecting how their overweight cat seemed to perpetually scrounge for food in the kitchen. Like it had Anne, RIZALTID had now killed this innocent creature. A hard resolve was beginning to form in Steven to bring the corporation to account.

And he was sure the MultiNutriGood canister in the garbage bag held proof of the cause of Anne's death, the senseless death caused by RIZALTID corporate management's negligent greed. Steven paused to think about his next step. How could he confirm the MNG was contaminated and bring that evidence to the attention of the corporate hierarchy?

Maybe he could use the corporation's help for that, he thought, but he needed a sample to test. Steven carefully left the garbage bag on the kitchen floor and went to the bathroom medicine cabinet to look for pill bottles for a suitable sample container.

Anne doesn't need that anymore, he thought angrily, as he took one of her prescription bottles with a childproof cap and emptied its contents into another one. Then he went back to the kitchen, taking another set of gloves, and carefully reopened the MNG canister to tip out a small amount of powder into the prescription bottle.

Putting the pill bottle aside, he resealed everything else including the body of poor Whiskers in the garbage bag he'd dispose of as carefully as possible. Then, he carefully applied tape to the pill bottle containing the powder sample to ensure it wouldn't leak. He knew where the labs were in the headquarters building and surely one of the chemists could and would check the powder for him.

Thursday morning, he called Amelia again to tell her he would be late but should get to work sometime in the morning. As it turned out, apparently even corporation scientists in labs on the fifth floor of the headquarters building were disaffected by the corporation's upper echelons, so getting his powder sample tested was easier than he anticipated once he got past the preliminaries.

Randy Johnson, another face he vaguely knew from the cafeteria, was the first chemist he encountered when he entered the lab area. "I'm not sure I understand," Johnson said.

"You have this substance you want tested, and you think it might be highly toxic, but you're awfully vague about where it came from and why you think it could be." He looked at Steven with a quizzically arched eyebrow waiting for an explanation.

Three brief sentence exchanges later, Steven blurted out his suspicion and the explanation for careful handling of the sample.

"Jesus!" Johnson exclaimed looking at the sealed pill bottle. "If this is what you think, it's going to take very special handling. Why are you bringing this to me off the books so to speak rather than officially through the Admin offices? If what you suspect is true people up there need to know about this."

"I think they already know," Steven replied, "or at least the higher-ups do. From what I've heard I believe they did their best to cover up the whole thing and think they succeeded. If I tried to take this to Admin, they'd deny anything could be wrong, particularly when the autopsy toxicology report for my wife didn't detect any toxic substances, and then they'd make the sample disappear so there wouldn't be any proof."

"Fuck. If it's that MX-21c stuff mixed in with this, the medical examiners wouldn't even know how to test for it." Johnson shook his head. "Fuckers," he said, startling Steven with his vehemence. "You're right. That's just the way the dark forces upstairs would do things here. So, let me ever-so-carefully test this and I'll let you know the results by early next week. This is explosive shit and I need to do this quietly, but I have a couple of other members of the rebel alliance here in the lab who will be willing to help. I'll get the analysis done quietly and get back to you with the results. Let me have your contact info."

They exchanged contact information and Steven went back down to his job in Food Services to wait for Johnson's analysis.

• • •

The next Tuesday came, and so did a call from Randy Johnson. The tone of the call was odd, though, with Johnson speaking in an almost jovial manner as if he and Steven knew each other well. "Hey, buddy, you up for lunch at the place in town we talked about?"

"Uh, yeah. I mean yes, I am. What time?"

"If you can swing it with your boss, meet me in parking lot P-3 around 11:20 or so? Let her give you a long lunch break so we can go to that great Mexican place I told you about that has the killer food."

At the word 'killer' Steven froze and sat there, phone in hand, quietly stunned.

"Steve? Buddy? You there? Will that work for you?"

"Um, yeah, I'll make it work. See you at 11:20."

The drive to the restaurant and ordering and eating their meals had a surrealistically normal aspect. That aside, Steven had to admit the Mexican food was indeed killer. "This is the best I've had since I moved here from San Diego," he said as he and Randy finished their meals.

"Yup, it is great," Johnson agreed. Then he looked around the restaurant carefully, reached into his coat, and pulled out a folded piece of paper he slid across the tabletop to Steven. "Cutting to the chase, that's your analysis," he said in a low voice. "Bottom line is you were right about MX-21c being mixed in with the MultiNutriGood. The amount of MX-21c in the sample we tested would be an exceptionally toxic dose."

"How toxic?" Steven asked quietly.

"Very. A tablespoon of that mixture would contain enough MX-21c to kill any healthy human being, and it would probably happen pretty quickly, say within 10 minutes, as the poison got into the bloodstream and spread throughout the body."

"Could it cause a brain hemorrhage?" Steven asked.

"I'm not sure exactly, but that's possible," Randy replied. "Is that what happened to your wife?" Steven nodded mutely.

"Well, fuck, I'm sorry about that." Randy shook his head and took a deep breath before going on. "Here's the thing, though: because of its formulation, the MX-21c isn't going to show up in any normal tox screening during an autopsy. A coroner would have to know about MX-21c, which is highly unlikely given the proprietary nature of the formula and how new it is, and he'd have to suspect its presence to order a complex test with highly specific parameters to detect the stuff in a human corpse. That is so unlikely it would actually have been surprising if he had found it in your wife's body."

"And she's been cremated so there's nothing more of her body left to test now anyway."

"Yeah, that, too. I honestly do sympathize with you, Steven," Johnson went on. "This is really fucked up, but the other thing is, I'm selfish and like my job, so you have to keep me and the other rebels out of anything you say upstairs in our building. That's part of the reason I've brought this to you in a kind of secret agent way. I don't know where you plan to go with this now, but I wish you luck Steven, and hope you get satisfaction somehow." Johnson reached across the table offering his hand and Steven took it to shake. "Be careful."

Steven nodded at that.

•   •   •

It took Steven the rest of the day to do it, but he managed to schedule an appointment with the Vice President for Human Resources the next day, Wednesday afternoon. Considering it was that VP's initiative that led to the contaminated MulitNutriGood being distributed to HQ employees, even if he did it without knowing about the toxic contamination, he was the person Steven most strongly wanted to confront and hold responsible for Anne's death.

•   •   •

The next afternoon, Steven was ushered into the Vice President's office only twenty minutes after the time of his appointment.

Reginald Gessler, the VP in question, was a member of the family that owned RIZALTID. "You're Brooks," he said looking up from a file on his desk after Steven was seated.

"Yes, sir."

"I'm Reginald Gessler, but I believe you know that already." Steven nodded.

Gessler looked down at the file then back up, saying, "Your wife died recently I understand?"

Steven felt a pang of sorrow as he replied, "Yes, that's what I wanted to talk to you about."

"I want you to know you have RIZALTID's deepest condolences at the tragic loss of your wife Isabel."

"Anne."

"What?"

"Her name was Anne," Steven corrected Gessler.

"Are you sure? The file we have says her name was Isabel. I guess that doesn't matter," Gessler went on before Steven could interject again, "This," he said tapping the file, "says you have a daughter named Sally?"

"Yes, I do."

"Well, there you go," Gessler said and closed file. "I presume you received the death benefit paid out from our insurance company. We like to make sure our employees are taken care of."

Steven shook his head. "I haven't actually received it yet; the Insurance firm says it is still processing the claim, but it should be paid soon."

"That's all right then. I'm sure you can understand we have to be careful with our money. Now, what can I do for you?"

"It's about the bonus you arranged to be distributed to headquarters employees, the MultiNutriGood supplement. I have evidence it was contaminated with an industrial poison produced by RIZALTID called MX-21c. My wife had some of the contaminated MNG and that killed her."

Gessler frowned and shook his head. "That can't be true," he insisted. "Out of an abundance of caution we recovered all that batch of MNG." Steven began to speak but Gessler waved him to silence. "It was all tested by our scientists, and it all tested out safe for human consumption."

"But that can't be true," Steven protested, certain the part about scientists testing the MNG was corporate cover-your-ass bullshit. "There's enough conversational buzz about the foul up on the product lines I'm sure that part is true. And the headquarters internal program status shows both production lines were shut down at the same time the bonus canisters were handed out, and those lines are still currently shut down. Something was definitely wrong involving both the MultiNutriGood and MX-21c. I have my evidence, and I want RIZALTID to do the right thing here."

"You do, do you?" Gessler glared at Steven. "I can see what this is about now. The insurance wasn't enough money for you and now you're trying to extort more money out of the corporation with your contrived evidence."

"It's not about money," Steven said firmly. "I want RIZALTID to acknowledge its fault and to make sure this doesn't happen again."

Gessler scoffed. "You want to know what the right thing is for a corporation to do? It's to maximize profits. We," he said with an expansive wave taking in the headquarters building and factory complex, "are in business here, and the whole point of business is making money. You know how I know that? I'm a business school graduate. Wharton if you must know," Gessler said with a hand pointing at a wall full of certificates. "What's your degree in?"

"I don't have a college degree."

"Right. Here's something for you to think about, Brooks: when you accuse the corporation of wrongdoing, do you know who you're accusing? Me and the rest of my family who own RIZALTID."

He eyed Steven shrewdly. "It always comes down to money though. So, you're here either trying to extort more money from me or establish the basis for a lawsuit. I'll tell you," he said jabbing a finger at Steven, "you need to think very carefully about doing either of those things. Isabel's death wasn't RIZALTID's fault." Steven felt a rising anger with Gessler's denial and getting Anne's name wrong again as if her name and being were inconsequential.

"We have our evidence and lawyers to most strongly assert our innocence in this matter. You don't want to challenge us. Neither you nor your daughter would do well if you pursue this further.

"In any case, you have a choice: drop this or be fired. Good luck finding a job if you're fired. Choose wisely for your sake and that of you daughter. I'm sure you know the right thing to do now."

Gessler pressed a buzzer to summon his assistant. "We're done here."

•   •   •

Steven found himself somewhat brusquely ushered out of the VP's office in a state of deepening anger. He stumbled to the elevator bank and rode one back down to the sub level where he worked in the headquarters building Food Services Division. He walked back toward the Food Services offices and stopped outside as his shock turned to turmoil then outrage in his mind.

Anger simmered inside him, anger at his wife's senseless death, anger at the corporation's lack of human concern, anger that Gessler had made the issue so much about money rather than Steven's honest concerns, and anger at the way Gessler had spoken to him and threatened him and Sally. Steven felt an overwhelming compulsion to act, to pay back RIZALTID for what it had done to his family.

No, it wasn't a faceless RIZALTID that had harmed his family, he realized, it was the fucking family members who owned the corporation who needed to face justice. He paused in his thinking, wondering what the hell he could possibly do from his position?

Steven shook his head, pushed the outer door open, and then stepped into the office section still fuming from thoughts of the meeting with Gessler. He paused when he heard a barely audible sound coming from the direction of his boss's small office. He frowned, trying to recognize the sound before he strode over to the partly opened door and looked in.

Amelia Roberts was slumped in her desk chair making quietly sorrowful sounds. Steven knocked on the doorframe and pushed the door the rest of the way open. Amelia jerked up at the sound and spun in her chair to look at Steven. She hurriedly pushed herself up and stood erect a few feet from him and wiped a tear from her cheek.

Steven took a tentative step toward her and asked, "What's wrong?"

Amelia shook her head, "It's nothing."

"I know you well enough to be able to tell it's not 'nothing,' Amelia. Tell me what's going on, please."

Amelia stood there looking at his earnest face for a moment, then nodded. "You're right, it is something. You know I'm not one to complain and I try to stay positive about our work here, but this is too much, so you get to hear me vent.

"It's the fucking family members who own RIZALTID," she went on. "They're holding their quarterly owners meeting in a couple of days and want me to serve and wait on them at their executive dining room on the thirty-first floor."

Steven nodded his understanding of that and made a 'go on' gesture with his hand.

"Well," Amelia took in a deep breath, "when I've been required to do this in the past those people, they're all men you know?" Steven nodded. "Well, they've been crude and disgusting. They leer at me, make suggestive comments, and there's a certain amount of inappropriate touching that goes on. The amount and degree of touching just depend on how quick and agile I am, but I have to bend over the table to serve and carry empty plates away, so that gives them their chances anyway. Our boss just reminded me the board members specifically want me serving them and that they want me to be wearing a 'cute little skirt' this time rather than the slacks I've worn before. You can imagine why they want me in a skirt."

"Can't you go to HR and complain?"

"No," she said, shaking her head. "You know how they've been replacing human workers with AI-controlled robots? Well, that's just one more piece of evidence that proves RIZALTID doesn't give a rat's ass about workers in the company. If I complain or refuse, I risk losing my job here. But I need a job, and I need healthcare for my family and myself. I can't afford to lose this job. All that was just too much for a moment, and my reaction to it was what you walked in on."

Thinking back on his just-concluded meeting, Steven nodded his understanding of the position she was in and the likely lack of concern for her complaints by an office that didn't even care if people could die from a factory mix-up. "And you can't just quit for some reason and move on?" he asked.

Amelia scoffed and answered, "No, that's the hell of it. I'm effectively trapped here in RIZALTID's employ. Did you read the fine print in your contract?" He shook his head. "Well, neither did I. It was a long form with lots of legalese, and I mean, who reads the fine print anyway, right?"

Steven nodded.

"Well, I have a non-compete clause in mine. If I quit, I can't engage in the same business, the culinary work I trained for, which is my vocation, within one hundred and fifty miles of this RIZALTID location. So, I'd have to move. Moving means giving up my home and uprooting my family, then trying to find a job with pay and benefits as good as this one. You probably know from your own job search before you were hired here that wouldn't be easy to do."

Steven nodded again at that.

"The people up there," she nodded her head toward the upper floors of senior management, "collar and leash us to this job. They know exactly what they're doing, and they don't give a shit. So, I have to put up with the shit I go through when they hold their quarterly luncheon upstairs. At least it's just once every three months."

Amelia was right, Steven thought.

He could see now that what had made the job so attractive, its all-inclusive nature with healthcare, investment, and life insurance through convenient company subsidiaries, was a trap tying him and other employees tightly to an uncaring corporation run by uncaring owners. The anger lingering from his meeting with Gessler and the anger he felt about the casually overt mistreatment of Amelia boiled over into a resolve in Steven's mind as he thought about his dead wife, Amelia, and RIZALTID.

A decision crystallized in his mind. "I'll do it," he said.

"What?"

"I said I'll do it. I'll prepare and serve the luncheon. You've trained me, I'm confident I can do the job, and I have a special idea for this luncheon." He gave her a serious look and lightly placed his hands on her shoulders. "You just call in sick with some illness that means you are absolutely unable to come back to work until next week. That will at least give you a break this time," Steven said, "and maybe something can be done for the future."

Amelia looked into his eyes intently. "You're sure about this? I know you have the skill and work ethic, but those guys are bastards."

"I'm sure they are, but the level of bastardry will probably be less with me."

Amelia nodded and smiled. "Thank you," she said and leaned in to hug him for a moment before pulling away. "The meeting and luncheon are Friday, so I'm going home 'sick' now, leaving you in charge." She went back to her desk to begin gathering her things.

Steven turned and left Amelia's office, thinking about what he would prepare. It would be a hot summer day outside, he mused, so a meal best served cold would be ideal. He smiled grimly as he began to compile a list of ingredients.

•   •   •

Friday at noon, three months to the day after Anne had died, Steven rolled a large cart loaded with the meal he had prepared into the executive dining room on the thirty-first floor of the RIZALTID headquarters building.

The VP of HR looked at him with a frown and said, "I see you're here rather than the delectable Amelia. Where is Amelia? We were especially looking forward to seeing her." Others at the table grinned and snickered at that.

"I'm sorry, but she's very sick and unable to come to work today. She asked me to prepare a meal and serve you in her place."

"Hmmmpf. That can't be helped then, can it? Well, we can have her next time then. What was your name again?"

"Steven. Steven Brooks."

"Oh, yes. I remember now. Damn shame about your wife, Isabel, but there really wasn't anything we could have done. I'm glad to see our understanding holds and you've kept your job."

"Anne," Steven muttered under his breath, before speaking up. "Yes, I'm very glad I kept my job. May I serve you now?"

The family members nodded and motioned for Steven to fill their plates. He listened to the men bantering about RIZALTID profits and how each planned on spending his exorbitant share as he went around the table sand quickly filled each plate with the special cold dish he had prepared for this luncheon.

The plates quickly emptied as the family members ate while making remarks to each other about how tasty the food was. Reginald Gessler finished his own food after several minutes, sat back, coughed briefly and cleared his throat, then turned to Steven to compliment him on the meal.

"Thank you," Steven replied.

"What is this main dish you served? I don't recognize it, but it was incredibly tasty."

"I call it 'Revenge'," Steven said.

"Revenge?" chuckled Gessler. "Why Revenge?" he asked. "There has to be a story behind that."

The others turned to look expectantly at Steven, waiting to hear what he had to say.

"I named it Revenge," Steven said with a thin smile, "because 'revenge is a dish best served cold.' I think I have that quote right."

Reginald frowned at that and coughed again for a moment before and wheezing out, "What the hell are you talking about Brooks?"

"You said you liked the flavor? That dish was seasoned to mask the flavor of a special additive I included, a RIZALTID product. There were a couple of tablespoons worth of MultiNutriGood powder for each plate I served today.

"That MNG in your meals today is from the first batch run you used as a cheap bonus for employees here in the headquarters three months ago. It was the batch with toxic MX-21c contamination that killed my wife," Steven said with a grim look on his face. "The corporation was responsible for that, and, as was pointed out to me two days ago, you seven here are the Corporation. That makes you seven guilty of my wife's death."

"All that food was safe," Reginald Gessler weakly protested through labored breathing and another coughing fit that wracked his body.

"That wasn't true. You knew it," Steven said, pointing an accusing finger around the room, "and the rest of you did, too. That's why you tried to cover it up with bullshit evidence that 'proved' the entire first batch was 'safe for human consumption'."

Steven looked around the exquisite dining room at family members who were all gasping for breath now as their bodies began to tremble in a precursor to the painful convulsions they would experience soon. "Well, now you've gotten to figuratively eat those words. The MNG in the food I served you came from a contaminated food canister I brought home to my wife and inadvertently kept after she died."

"You see, my wife wanted to try the MNG in a protein shake as soon as I brought it home," Steven continued. "From what I know, she died in agony about seven or eight minutes after ingesting the contaminated MNG in her shake." He glanced at his watch. "So, given the amount of time it's been since you began eating, I believe you only have a couple of minutes left to live now."

He looked back up at the seven family members. "My wife's name was Anne, not Isabel, and you killed her," he said. "Think about that. And then, gentlemen, you can all go to hell."

Steven stood with folded arms watching Dr. Williams' graphic description of the final moments of Anne's life play out before him as each family member was showing obvious signs of the effect of their hemorrhaging brain tissues. Reginald, the youngest family member and last one served, struggled to push himself up from his chair and stood momentarily before collapsing to the plush carpeted floor. The other six made feeble trembling efforts to move but failed to rise from their seats.

Steven stepped over to Reginald Gessler's twitching form and squatted to look him in the eye. Gessler stared back with a panic-stricken look as he struggled to draw each last wheezing breath.

"See," Steven pointed out conversationally, "you lied about the contaminated MNG. I told the truth."

He watched the life fade from Reginald's eyes, then stood up and looked around the table. When the last body stilled from its final convulsion, Steven calmly went around the table collecting plates and tableware to load back onto the serving cart. With all the plates, silverware, and glassware collected, Steven observed the scene one last time, nodded with satisfaction, then turned his back on the former RIZALTID Corporation owners. He pushed the cart from the dining room, humming his wife's favorite tune as he went.

About the Author

Bob Schoonover is a Navy brat, with a Navy pilot father and Navy WAVE mother. He moved frequently as a child until his father retired and settled in Chico, California in the '60s.

After high school in Chico and attending Occidental College, Bob began his own career in the Navy as a Naval Flight Officer trained for P-3 Orion patrol planes (a land-based aircraft conducting anti-submarine warfare missions and search and rescue). He served at permanent duty stations in Hawaii and San Diego with deployments to the Western Pacific and Indian Ocean. Bob met and married his wife, also a Navy officer, in Hawaii.

After Bob retired, he followed his wife during the remainder of her career to assignments leading to Newport, Rhode Island where they reside with three cats. During his post-Navy career, Bob has been a house husband to their only child since her age of seven, substitute high school teacher, and a high school track and cross-country coach. Bob is an accomplished watercolor artist and copper wire sculptor of wildlife. He has been a scribbler his whole life and is now writing fiction as a vocation.

You Might Also Enjoy

Parrish Blue
by Vanessa MacLaren-Wray

Sallie never expected to discover a world she'd forgotten how to imagine.

Reduction in Force
by Steve Soult

A heartless corporate layoff leaves Gil Schaffer emotionally shattered.

Saying Goodbye
by J Dark

A young girl, searching for the parents who abandoned her, discovers that some answers only lead to more questions.

Available in digital and trade paperback editions from
Water Dragon Publishing
waterdragonpublishing.com